USE

BLACK
SPOT FOUND

BIG BILL

BE'ARD
PIRATE
BE APPROACHED

DREADFUL
DR. DULL

REWARD
FOR INFORMATIO
LEADING TO ARRES

IVAN
ZEGOLD

LY

PETE
BULL

SMALL, BUT DEADLY

LADY GARGOYLE

WANTED FOR
PIRAC

GEORGE 'JAWS'
CAUTION: MAY BITE

WANTED

~the~
BEASTLY PIRATES
John Kelly
BLOOMSBURY
LONDON NEW DELHI NEW YORK SYDNEY
the PIRATE'S END
CLUB TONITE!
FOR SALE! CLASSIC CANNON - ONE CARELESS OWNER.

There's a tavern by the harbour
and it's called
The Pirate's End,
where the **roughest** rogues sit swapping
tales of **terror** with their friends.

They talk of Roger Ramrod
who **stole** the old Queen's fillings,
and Wicked Cass, the pirate lass,
who'd **slice** you for a shilling.

"I remember," one exclaims,
through halitosis breath,
"the **scariest pirate** that ever lived –
they called him **Captain Death!**"

"Pure hogwash!" snarls another,
"I knew tiny Admiral Flea.
He'd stroll below a cutlass blow
and stab you in the knee."

They babble on for hours
with their tales of **fear** and **dread**,
until the sleepy serving boy
climbs **up** the stairs to bed.

Then, with a shudder, one **dares** mention
(quietly at first)
the gang of **cut-throats** known by all
to be the **very worst**.

They're called
The Beastly Pirates
and this **fearsome** ugly bunch
scour the seas for other pirates
they can **gobble** up for lunch.

They claim there's nothing better
than a **tasty pirate snack.**
So when they hear a
Yo Ho Ho!
they sail in and attack.

The **Beastly Captain Snapper**
is most **hideous** and **vile.**
A one-eyed, cutlass-toting,
pirate-eating crocodile.

With a body **hard** and **muscled,**
covered head to toe in **scales,**
his **colossal** snout is four feet long,
and full of **teeth** like **nails.**

Bosun Beastly loves bananas
but will always take a **bite**
of any **salty sea-dog**
he's defeated in a fight.

His victims try to flee and hide,
they **blub** and **sob** and **squeal**,
but always end up at the Bosun's
'**special**' three-course **meal**.

The **Beastlies** ate Old Stinky,
the **whiffiest** man afloat,
whose **smell** was so **revolting** that
his crew had its own boat.

He was chomped up by the **Scurvy Dog**,
who did seem rather pleased,
and claimed that **Stinky** tasted
just like **Gorgonzola cheese.**

Admiral Archibald the Angry
had such dreadful fits of rage
that his crew were used to locking him
securely in a cage.

But **Snapper** yanked the bars apart
and set the Admiral free.
Then **polished off** his crew
with buttered crumpets and sweet tea.

Bald bullet-headed **Ivor Shot**
lived for the cannon's **roar,**
but thought that aiming carefully
was something of a **bore.**

Krusher Kraken squeezed him
in a tentacle or two,

and served him with spaghetti
and a very nice ragu.

That two-tonne terror, **Captain Blimp**,
was **greedy**, **fat** and **cruel**.
He **gobbled** up his sailors' grub
and only served them gruel.

The Beastlies baked him in a pie,
and not a bit was wasted,
with crispy crust and gravy –
quite the best they'd ever tasted!

Now all these **beastly tales**
leave the tavern pirates **spooked**.
They've started thinking one day
they could end up getting **cooked!**

Then, all at once, the quiet dark
is broken by a
THUMP!
And every pirate heartbeat
does an unexpected jump!

"Is there **something** on the landing?"
Did they hear a **moan** or scrape?
The candlelight upon the stairs
reveals a **ghastly** shape.

Aaaaaaagh!
"THE B-B-BEASTLIES!"
cry the pirates,
as the shadow fills the room.
"Help! Won't someone save us from
our grisly, gruesome DOOM?"

"Oi there! What's this racket?"
cries the figure with the light.
"Do you **pirates** have the slightest clue
how **late** it is at **night**?

The Beastlies is a tale that's told
to **pirate** girls and boys,
to make them **eat up** all their greens
and tidy up their toys.

Now off you go. It's time for bed.
and **don't** you make a peep.
Some of us would **really** like
to get a good night's sleep!"

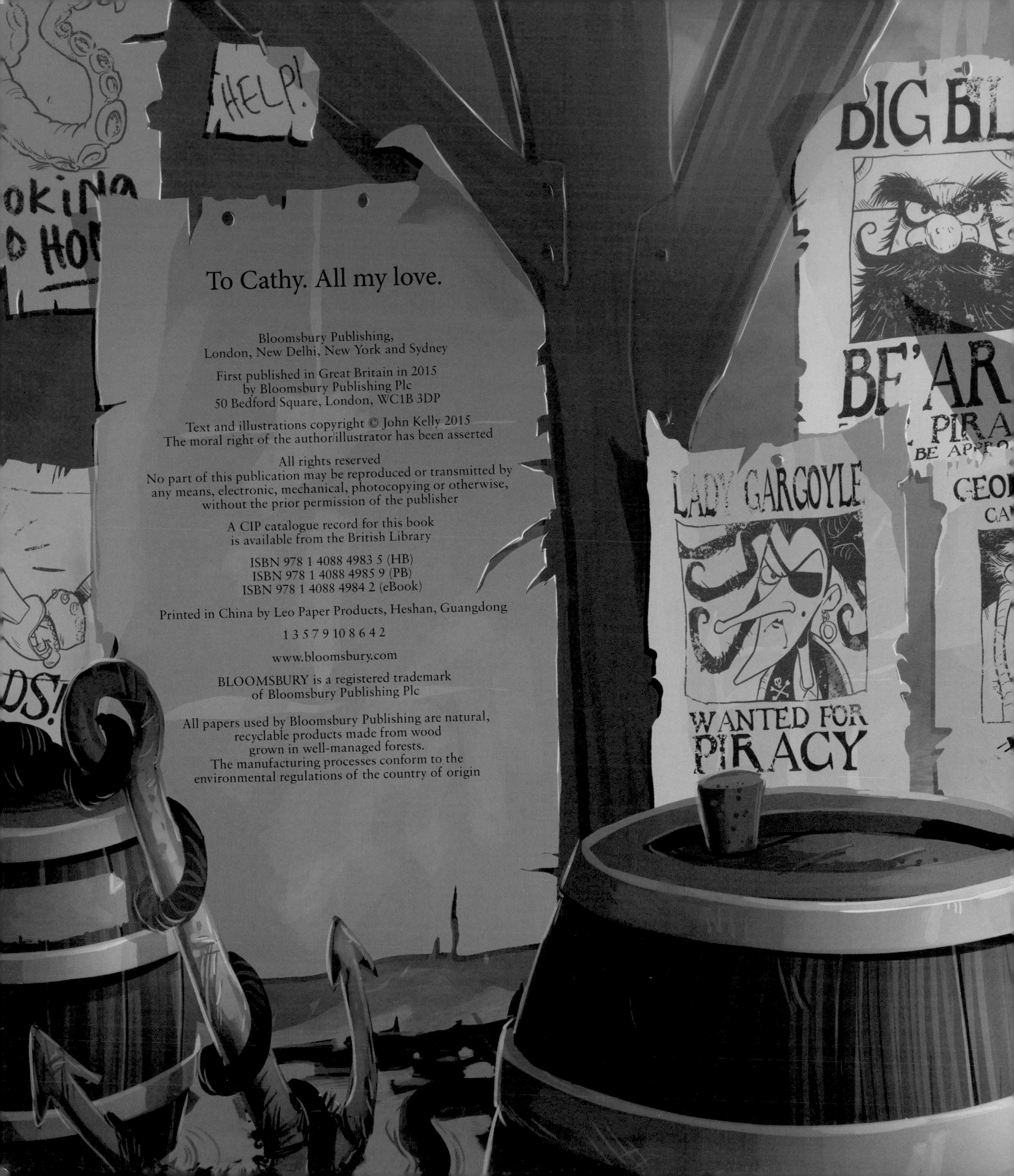

To Cathy. All my love.

Bloomsbury Publishing,
London, New Delhi, New York and Sydney

First published in Great Britain in 2015
by Bloomsbury Publishing Plc
50 Bedford Square, London, WC1B 3DP

A CIP catalogue record for this book
is available from the British Library

ISBN 978 1 4088 4983 5 (HB)
ISBN 978 1 4088 4985 9 (PB)
ISBN 978 1 4088 4984 2 (eBook)

Printed in China by Leo Paper Products, Heshan, Guangdong

1 3 5 7 9 10 8 6 4 2

www.bloomsbury.com

BLACK SPOT FOUND
DREADFUL DR. DULL
IVAN ZEGOLD
PETE BULL
SMALL, BUT DEADLY
FOR SALE! CLASSIC CANNON
– ONE CARELESS OWNER